MR. PRICKLES

PRICKLES

A QUILL-FATED LOVE STORY

KARA LaREAU / PICTURES BY SCOTT MAGOON

A NEAL PORTER BOOK
ROARING BROOK PRESS
NEW YORK

For Neal, my pal in prickliness —K.L.

For Jim and Jean, a loving pair —S.M.

Text copyright © 2012 by Kara LaReau
Illustrations copyright © 2012 by Scott Magoon
A Neal Porter Book
Published by Roaring Brook Press
Roaring Brook Press is a division of Holtzbrinck Publishing Holdings Limited Partnership
175 Fifth Avenue, New York, New York 10010
mackids.com

Library of Congress Cataloging-in-Publication Data
LaReau, Kara..
Mr. Prickles : a quill-fated love story / Kara LaReau ; illustrations by
Scott Magoon. — 1st ed.
p. cm.
"A Neal Porter book."
Summary: Excluded by the other forest animals for not being cute, cuddly,
and playful, a porcupine feels lonely and angry until he finds a prickly
companion, Miss Pointypants.
ISBN 978-1-59643-483-7
[1. Porcupines—Fiction. 2. Forest animals—Fiction. 3.
Friendship—Fiction.] I. Magoon, Scott, ill. II. Title. III. Title: Mister
Prickles.
PZ7.L55813Mr 2012
[E]—dc22

2010045188

Roaring Brook Press books are available for special promotions and premiums.
For details contact: Director of Special Markets, Holtzbrinck Publishers.

First edition 2012
Book design by Jennifer Browne
Printed in the United States of America by Worzalla, Stevens Point, Wisconsin

3 5 7 9 8 6 4

Mr. Prickles was not a particularly friendly fellow.

Much of his unfriendliness
was due to the fact that
Mr. Prickles was a porcupine.

By their very nature,
porcupines are very hard
to get close to.

At first, Mr. Prickles tried to make friends
with the other animals in the forest.

He tried to join in their nightly frolicking, but it was fruitless.

He tried to join in their midnight picnicking,

but it was pointless.

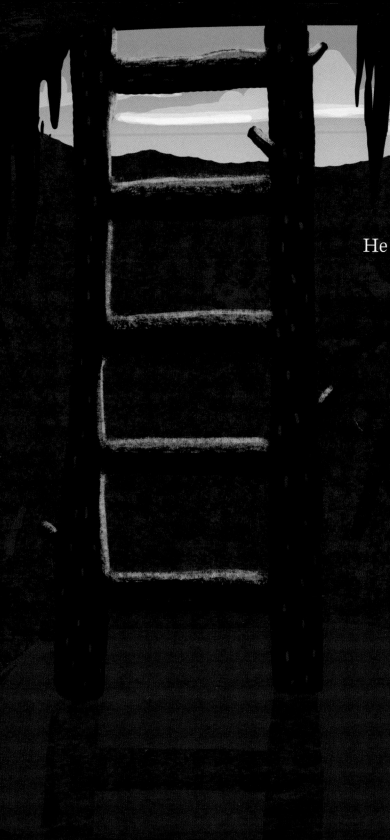

He tried to join in their daily sleepover,

but he was clearly unwelcome.

The others always said the same thing.

"You're not cute like us," said Raccoon.

"Or cuddly like us," said Chipmunk.

"Or playful like us," said Skunk.

"I am," said Mr. Prickles. "On the inside."

But no one would believe him.

The more the other
animals avoided
Mr. Prickles,
the more
lonely
he felt.

Very lonely.

He began to feel angry.

He even began 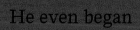 to feel prickly on the inside.

Very prickly.

Each night, as the other animals frolicked in the forest,
Mr. Prickles watched them from his stump
with very prickly regard.

Unfortunately, the other animals
didn't seem to care.

"Porcupines are so unfriendly,"
said Raccoon.

"Not to mention dangerous," said Chipmunk.

"And *not* like us," reminded Skunk.

One night, as Mr. Prickles was glaring at the other animals,

he noticed another porcupine in the stump next to his.

"My name is Miss Pointypants," said the porcupine.

"My name is Mr. Prickles," said Mr. Prickles.

They knew better than to try and shake hands.
Instead, they regarded each other pointedly.

Each night after that, Mr. Prickles and Miss Pointypants
would watch the frolicking animals with equally prickly regard.
"All this glaring is boring," Miss Pointypants said, finally.

"You're right," said Mr. Prickles.

"Let's go," she said. "We can't let them have all the fun."

So the porcupines left their stumps
and went out for a stroll.

They swam and splashed in the cool, dark lake.

They dined on twigs and bark and clover and cabbage.

They watched the moon rise over the water.

"It feels nice to be out, doesn't it?" Miss Pointypants said.

"Very nice," said Mr. Prickles.

On the way home, the porcupines ran into the other animals.

"Well, if it isn't Spike and Barb," said Raccoon.

"Looking sharp," said Chipmunk. "*Painfully* sharp."

"How do porcupines hug?" said Skunk. "Very carefully!"

Fortunately, the porcupines didn't seem to care.

"Whew! Their jokes stink," said Miss Pointypants.

"They're not as much fun as I thought they were," said Mr. Prickles.

"Or as funny," said Miss Pointypants.

"I don't feel quite so prickly anymore," Mr. Prickles said.

"On the inside, anyway."

"Me, neither," said Miss Pointypants.
It's much nicer being alone with someone else,
Mr. Prickles realized.

And most important, he learned that porcupines do hug, very carefully.

And *very* often.